WICKED

DEVILS POINT WOLVES

ELIZA GAYLE

GYPSY INK BOOKS

BE THE FIRST

Make sure you sign up for my newsletter for all the up-to-date book news, FREE books, and lots of behind the scenes goodies.

elizagayle.com/newsletter

PRO TIP: Make sure you add eliza@elizagayle.com to your contacts list to ensure the newsletter goes straight to your inbox.

ABOUT THE BOOK

Wicked
The Mating Season Collection
by Eliza Gayle
Published by Gypsy Ink Books, © 2015 Eliza Gayle

All Rights Reserved

eliza@elizagayle.com
http://ElizaGayle.com
Eliza on Instagram - @elizagayleauthor
Eliza on Facebook - authorelizagayle
Eliza on Tiktok - @elizagayleauthor
Sign up for Eliza's Newsletter

WICKED: Devils Point Wolves #2

Fueled by revenge, driven by need. This mating season won't go down easy.

Rebel has one last thing to do before she can walk away from her life on Devils Point and the man she can't get out of her head. Find the shifter who hurt her sister. She'll have to work with Dante to make it happen and that might be the final straw that breaks her. Unless she can come up with an idea to get him out of her system. Like one night of no holds barred sex. Hot, dirty and thoroughly... Yeah, she definitely needs to get her mind out of the gutter.

Dante thought he was waiting for his mate. It's what they were taught and what every wolf yearns for. But this mating season brought him a different kind of woman. Curvy, feisty and downright wicked. She is also not his true mate and everyone thinks he should let her go. Too bad she's under his skin and he doesn't know what to do about it. Well...he actually does have some ideas about *that*.

ante repeated the name in his head as soon as the host announced the next dancer to hit the stage at Club Diablo, all while contemplating the ways he could make her pay.

Rebel.

She strutted on stage and he got lost in the sight of her. Leather vest over a leather micro mini skirt, boots up to her thighs, all revealing the creamy flesh he couldn't keep his hands off no matter how hard he tried.

She'd changed her hair from its original frothy blonde color to a fire engine red. It did not change the level of magnetism he felt looking at her. In fact, it might have made it worse. Red drew the eye and it caught his attention as he watched it cascade down her back and skim the top of her ass. Did he mention what a fantastic ass she had? Dante swallowed a groan. He already knew what it felt like to have his hands cupped around those perfect cheeks and he wanted it again. She might be the twin to his brother's mate, Faith, but in his mind they looked nothing alike.

They were night and day. Light and dark. Wicked and sweet.

His body tightened the more he thought of her until his pants grew uncomfortable and he wanted to drive into something. Preferably her.

Except for the past two weeks she'd kept her distance. Not an actual physical distance since they'd spent a lot of time together trying to find the rogue wolf that bit her sister and the possible hunter that he was beginning to believe might have been a figment of his imagination. How else did he explain no sign of him for two weeks? People disappeared all the time, but Dante wasn't human and it wasn't easy for a human to disappear from a wolf without a trace. Every human carried a unique scent that allowed them to be easily tracked.

Rebel reached for the pole and the thoughts of hunters and rogues disappeared from his mind. Her hips rotated, making him think of sex again. Every thrust and grind as she whipped around the stage like it was nothing drove him higher. How many times had he seen her dance now? He'd lost track. But every time was like the first time as he began silently chanting in his head for her to take off her clothes.

The men around the stage were crowding closer, as they usually did. She was one of their most popular dancers. Hard not to be when she represented everything that one might dream a bad girl would be like. Beyond the new fiery hair and the tight leather clothes, Rebel had an air about her that anyone could guess came with a pretty big bite.

Maybe it was the tattoos that adorned parts of her. He'd never seen that much ink on a woman, but damn did it turn him on.

Apparently, whenever she traveled to a new place she liked to take home a permanent souvenir. He'd already memorized them all, but had yet to learn the story behind every one. He did know the sugar skull on her back was from a wild weekend in Mexico with some people she barely knew. And the wine bottle wrapped in thorns came from a month in California wine country with some rich guy that she claimed had a fetish for bad girls.

That was another thing about Rebel. She attracted everyone and made friends with nearly all of them. And yet, somehow managed to never let anyone get too close. Even her sister was forced to remain in her life from a distance.

Apparently Rebel didn't carry the twin gene that made them want to be connected at all times. Although he was pretty sure Faith did. It didn't take a genius to pick up the little nuances of the newest member of their pack.

Whenever she spent time with Rebel, her eyes filled with a sadness that pulled at everyone around her. She didn't think anyone noticed, but he did and so did Rebel.

Whatever was going on inside that women, she didn't like disappointing her sister. The loss of their parents a few years back had created some sort of rift between them and so far neither seemed to know how to fix it. Dante knew this because Damien was on a tear about trying to help them deal with it. His brother was a little nuts about doing whatever it took to make his new mate happy.

Pussy.

The thought of Damien convincing Rebel to do anything made Dante laugh. He couldn't imagine her welcoming any interference from his brother. She was still pissed at all of them. Two weeks back she'd walked into a fight between he and Damien that had resulted in him going wolf and scaring the hell out of her.

Not exactly how he'd wanted her to find out.

Rebel peeled her leather vest off and revealed generous breasts that were now bare except for the red pasties covering her nipples. His mouth watered. Rebel wasn't like most humans when it came to her body. She wasn't afraid to reveal it in any way and she seemed to revel in showing it off. Although when he asked her about it she said it was all about the money.

Club Diablo paid their dancers very well. As the main business that brought income to the island, it was important to them all to make sure the guests who came in were treated extremely well. By paying the dancers over the norm, they not only got the best talent, they didn't have a lot of turnover, which suited them perfectly. Although it wasn't easy to find strippers that appealed to shifters. They were aggressive and interested in women who were not stick thin. It took a little meat on the bones to handle sex with a wolf.

So they paid extra to find them.

Living on an island might make their pack feel isolated, in reality they weren't. They were surrounded on three sides by a peninsula with a variety of small towns from tiny to average. And with the city of Tacoma just a couple of bridges away, Washington didn't feel quite as big as it used to. In fact, with a hunter possibly wandering their lands and a rogue loose at the same time, the real world encroached far more than was comfortable.

Dante scanned the faces in the crowd watching Rebel's performance, looking for a hint of either the hunter or the rogue. All they had to go on was a description of the rogue in wolf form and the scent of the hunter that had more to do with their weapons than the actual person. His pack hated guns and their scent that permeated everything.

He stilled on one quickly becoming familiar face. He didn't know the man, but he recognized him as a repeat customer. Dante took a slow deep breath and filtered through the scents of the room. Not an easy feat with this many people this close and in an aroused state.

Above it all he scented Rebel though. A heady fragrance of jasmine from the lotion she kept in her purse and reapplied often, to the light sheen of sweat that made her body glisten under the lights. She was up on the pole now working it with the strong muscles of her inner thighs. He could easily imagine those long legs of hers wrapped around his waist as he drove into her. He ground his teeth to force down the growl that threatened. Watching her was easy enough, but knowing what went through the minds of the other men as they watched her wasn't. They wanted to fuck her too.

Dante sighed. This is why he and his brothers did not get involved with the dancers if they could help it. Mixing business with pleasure led to disastrous results. His brother, Diego had learned that the hard way when a human dancer wormed her way under his skin and then...

A sharp scent filtered through his scents and Dante jerked his head in the direction. A strong odor of metal. It disappeared as quickly as he scented it. He searched the room for the source. Was the hunter right here under his own nose? He growled, not bothering to hide it. A few of the shifter customers turned their heads and looked.

Either not interested in his business, or reluctant to get involved, they all slowly turned back to the show when they realized he stood nearby. As long as they weren't who he hunted, they had nothing to fear. He had no plans to screw up the good thing they had going here with Club Diablo. This establishment easily funded ninety percent of the island's operation, making it easier for the pack to keep to themselves instead of seeking employment off island.

There were other establishments that contributed to the welfare of the pack, like the diner and motel, but nothing compared to the Diablo. In recent years a few of the pack members had expressed concern about their sole source of income and initiatives had begun for other avenues of revenue. Some old school and some not.

They even had a dot com style start up that some of the pups were working on getting off the ground. Whatever they did was over his head. Other than the things they did online to market Club Diablo, he didn't have much use for technology other than the cell phone he carried around to keep in touch.

Some new catcalls from the stage area again caught his attention and he turned around just in time to see Rebel removing her skirt and throwing it above her head.

His mouth went dry. Like the pasties, the thong she wore was as red as her hair and the gloss she wore on her lips.

Fuck. He wanted to bite that scrap of silk off of her and bury his face between her thighs. They'd gone out a few times after hours as friends and each time things got a little more heated than he'd planned. Hard to stay in control when she seemed as eager as him to engage in some hot fucking sex.

He closed his eyes and reached deep for some shred of sanity that would keep him in place and not stalking to the stage and throwing her over his shoulder and taking her home.

That's what was killing him. This fucking mating season. That had to be why he couldn't stop thinking of laying hands on her. She'd made it perfectly clear she didn't want him anywhere near her anymore.

Unfortunately, everything that came out of her mouth these days filled him with rage. Like her half-baked plan to serve as bait for the rogue that bit her sister. He still couldn't believe that his pack agreed with her. Or that his brothers also went along with the idea.

Bastards.

As if she could hear his thoughts she turned her gaze to his on cue, giving him a look that clearly said fuck you. He clenched his jaw.

"You are a glutton for punishment." His brother Diego walked up next to him, a half smile across his face.

"You think that's funny?"

"Fuck yeah. She makes you squirm and that is a sight to behold."

Dante growled again. "You're supposed to be helping me find our rogue in the crowd not waste time giving me shit."

"I am an excellent multitasker."

It was then he noticed his brother's tight body language. To the casual observer he looked like nothing more than a man enjoying the show, but to him the subtle nuances such as the hard set of his jaw told Dante he was anything but a relaxed onlooker.

"Where's Damien?" he asked.

"Where do you think?" Diego smirked.

Dante sighed. Since turning his new mate wolf two weeks ago, they'd spent every waking moment running or fucking. He loved his brother and was happy he'd reconciled with his true mate, but this was mating season and it was driving them all a little crazier than usual it seemed.

"Any sign of our guy?"

Diego nodded his head. "Just that one dude to the right of the stage sitting in the shadows. His attention is fixated on Rebel, but he looks nervous. He fidgets a lot."

His brother had pointed out the same man he suspected, except he'd missed the nervous tics Diego easily discovered.

"We really going to do this? Just let her walk out of here unprotected?" he asked.

Diego shook his head. "She won't exactly be unprotected. Someone will have eyes on her the whole way."

"It only takes a second for this asshole to bite her or worse. Not even the fastest wolf in our pack will be able to stop that." And the thought of someone hurting her made him angry. A festering wound kind of anger that never relented.

"She's not exactly a pushover, dude."

"No match for a wolf."

Diego scoffed. "She has no problem taking you down."

"That's different." She'd grabbed his crotch and tried to neuter him. "She may not look like it on the outside, but she's vulnerable. And this is a bad idea."

Diego turned to him. "She made up her mind and she's determined. I agree that it's a dangerous thing for a human to take on. But I get why she needs to do it. You know as well as I do that you have to let her do this. Otherwise, she'll never trust the pack and you know we can't live with that."

Dante tried to ignore his brother's logic, but it was impossible. Without trust she'd have difficulty keeping their secrets. This wasn't what he hoped for her. He thought when she found out about his kind she'd be more on board. Everything he'd seen and learned about her said she had a very open mind.

"No, we can't have that," he admitted. There was no greater priority than keeping their existence a secret.

Especially now that extremists with more hate than logic, were turning hunters more and more these days.

"Any sign of the hunter?"

Diego shook his head.

"Someone took a shot at the wolf in front of Faith. And that bullet casing I found smelled like silver. Hunter or not someone knows something and they could fuck one of us up if they're screwing around."

Dante turned his attention back to the stage when he realized Rebel's music was beginning to fade. The fake smoke filled the front and all he saw was the swing of her wicked red hair and the sway of bare hips...

Diego walked closer and nudged his side. "Time to take our places, bro. Don't worry. She's going to be fine."

Dante frowned. "Isn't there a stupid saying about famous last words?"

TWO

Rebel flung open the dressing room door and crossed straight to the refrigerator on the back wall. She wasn't sure if she was amped up extra from two weeks off and she was already out of practice, or from the knowledge that the man she wanted to capture was likely watching her dance.

Either way she was on edge.

She grabbed a bottle of water and rubbed it along her face and neck in an attempt to cool off and slow her racing heartbeat. Of course there was a third option for her discomfort. As the men who fed bills into her G-string faded from her memory, only one man remained.

Dante.

Why couldn't she get over him? They were not in a relationship and they didn't even have sex. She sighed. It was sad she classified her time with men based on whether they had sex or not. Maybe though, that's all this was. Lust that needed to be fulfilled. It had been a while for her and she'd been thinking about going in that direction with him until that night... When she saw him change...

Since then she avoided him or avoided talking about what happened. The whole thing unnerved her.

So he was a shifter? Big fucking deal.

Except it was a big deal. Because they had all these mystical things like mating season and true mates that ruled their world. A place where she obviously didn't belong. Or should she say yet another place she couldn't belong?

She plopped down in the chair sitting in front of her dressing room table and stared in the mirror. Behind the stage make-up and what felt like a pound of glitter, she was still the same pathetic girl looking for that mysterious "thing" that eluded her. That feeling that would make her feel like her world had not actually been obliterated when her parents died and her twin left for college.

She'd begun to believe it was here on Devils Point. The chaos of Club Diablo mixed with the serenity of a small island seemed to make the perfect combination. She needed both. She lied to everyone about why she danced, making them think it was all about the money, when it wasn't. She loved to dance. It made her feel in control of her life.

Now she was closing in on the decision on whether she was going to stay or go. If tonight went well and they caught the asshole that attacked Faith, then she'd be free to leave. Her sister was settled in a big way with Damien and staying here only served to remind her on a daily—make that hourly—basis of what she could never have with Dante.

When she overheard him and Diego discussing Faith being their brother's true mate, she'd forced them to explain.

Oh boy. Be careful what you ask for...

That's the lesson she learned that night. She swiped a hand towel across her face, wishing she could wipe away the memories as easily as she did the sweat.

Apparently the wolves believed in and experienced some mystical connection when they bonded with their true mate. The person fated to them by some greater power. It made her insatiably curious about Dante's fate and so she confronted him with the question on whether he knew the identity of his true mate.

She'd seen the answer in his eyes before he bothered to respond.

No, he did not.

Which meant it wasn't her and no matter what happened between them, she would never be "the one."

Her shoulders sagged. Even thinking about it weeks later crushed her soul all over again. She put the water down on the table and grabbed her make-up wipes. She needed to shake it off and get her head on the real mission for tonight. Time to get the gunk off her face and get on with the rest of her life.

"You done for the night?" Melody, one of her fellow dancers came up behind her and watched her in the mirror.

"Yep. Just one tonight."

"Must be nice." She reached down and rubbed the side of her foot. "My feet are killing me."

Rebel grinned. "One of the many things we sacrifice to do this job." She grabbed her tube of foot rub and handed it to her friend. "Here, this will help."

"Thanks. A bunch of us are headed into Tacoma later tonight to hit one of the all night underground clubs. You want to go with?"

Ordinarily she would have been interested. The idea of getting a little lost in a night of partying sounded really good right about now. But tonight she hoped to catch that furry, human-biting asshole with her starring as the bait.

"Nah. Tired. Think I might be coming down with something."

Melody smiled. "Awww. That's too bad. But maybe Dante can come by your room tonight and kiss it all better."

She scrunched up her mouth in a lopsided frown. "Whatever."

Melody shook her head. "I don't see why not. It's obvious you two are crazy about each other. You should embrace it and jump him already. Either you have great sex and you get it out of your system, or you have great sex and realize you might have something together. It's pretty simple really. I'm not sure why people always want to make relationships so complicated."

Rebel stopped scrubbing her face and stared at Melody in the mirror. She made it sound so simple. And sex for sex's sake didn't sound like a bad thing. She certainly needed to do something to move on.

Melody wandered off to ask the other girls if they wanted to join her trip and Rebel turned back to her task at hand. Specifically, she needed to not waste much more time and get her butt out the back door of the club. If their planning panned out and this guy was as predictable as they suspected, he'd be waiting for her somewhere not far from the club. Either in the parking lot or on her walk to the motel, expecting easy prey.

For several nights now she'd gotten the sense that someone was watching her. Whenever she was alone, the hairs on the back of her neck would stiffen and goose bumps broke out across her arms. There was definitely someone out there and it was time to find out who.

She finished reapplying make-up more appropriate for outside the club and then cleaned up her table. She couldn't stand a messy area, to the point it drove her a little crazy until she fixed it. The only exception being her motel room when she went on a bender after finding out the guy she really liked was a werewolf. That had been a nightmare to clean up after.

She grabbed her clothes out of her locker and put them on. Short cutoff jeans, a white nearly sheer tank top and strappy sandals that made her tan legs look good while still being easy to run in. If that became necessary and she really hoped it didn't.

With one last glance in the mirror where she wiped a smudge of lip gloss from the corner of her mouth, she grabbed her purse and headed toward the employee exit.

There were live cameras that saw through the entire perimeter of the parking lot and they were betting on their rogue not only knowing about them, but also planning to avoid them when he made his move.

When she opened the door, the cool night breeze coming in off the water caught her breath. It never ceased to surprise her that no matter how hot it got on the island, the surrounding water always stayed cold. Made it easy to survive the summers here versus other places she lived, that's for sure.

She inhaled, taking a deep breath and pushed forward, letting the door close behind her. Every step she would make tonight had been planned out with Dante and his brothers and she knew that the entire pack was out here whether she could see them or not. They were here backing her up and planned to do whatever it took to keep her safe.

Still, her stomach trembled a little, making her all too aware that this mission she volunteered for could go south as easy as it could succeed. It all depended on how well she handled her part.

She walked across the parking lot, her body painfully alert as her muscles tensed the farther she moved away from the safety of the club. If she got through tonight she would definitely make a decision one way or the other about her future at Devils Point. There was no point to staying close by and torturing all of them any further if she needed to leave. A clean break would be the best course of action.

A cracking noise sounded to her left and Rebel froze.

THREE

The sound, while not overly loud in contrast to the club, boomed through her ears. While it could have been anything— Raccoon, squirrel, stray dog— the way her hackles rose told her it was more. Maybe one of the pack members?

More likely their rogue. He was smart but he made mistakes. And he was just as much affected by the mating season as Dante and the rest of his pack. More if he was feral.

Another scary shifter term she didn't particularly like. It sounded dangerous.

She kept going. There was nothing much she could do until he showed his face. They had to be sure it was him before they made their move. Since it wasn't entirely uncommon for a dancer to get followed home by one of her customers, it could be literally anyone. That was the downside to selling the illusion of sex. Some took the job far more serious than she did and thought if they tipped her high enough or if she showed them enough attention that they had some sort of claim on her.

They didn't and it only took a stern word or a hard grip on an arm from Damien, Dante or Diego to teach that lesson once. No one ever followed her more than once.

Until now.

As far as she could tell, this guy followed her a lot. She didn't always see him, but sensed his presence, and she trusted her instincts. She might not have superior shifter hearing or eyesight or smell, like most of the residents on this island, but she understood gut feelings and when she got them she didn't ignore them. Life was too dangerous not to pay attention when your brain was trying to tell you something.

You listen or you might die. Those might be scary thoughts to live by, but they were often true.

Once she cleared the parking lot, there were no more cameras or lights to discourage someone from pursuing her. That might have been all part of the plan, but the unease spurring her forward only escalated.

Despite having followed this path for more nights than she could count, and knowing that the pack had her back, Rebel's instinct was still to speed up and get home quicker. Fear crawled up her spine with each new step taken. This wasn't second thoughts about being bait, this was her fight or flight instinct pushing her to run.

Something was wrong.

She swung her head left and then right, searching for any sign of why she was so on edge. Shadows cast from the lights of the club swayed in the light breeze.

Her heartbeat sped up so fast her chest ached. And still she saw nothing more than the usual. Trees, soft leaf strewn ground with some grass growing between, and dirt that cushioned her walk.

Even though she was well away from the spotlights of the club there was still a lot of illumination. She looked up to see the fat, full moon shining down on her. Her fear turned bitter in her mouth, leaving a foul taste behind. Alone in the woods, waiting on a werewolf on a full moon. Maybe she hadn't thought through this stupid ass plan. There was a good chance she needed her head examined.

She quickened her pace, desperation beginning to set in. They could find another way to catch this guy. Another quarter of a mile and she would be out of the woods and on the small road that led to the tiny center of town. A quarter mile after that and she'd be well within spitting distance of the diner and across the road from the diner would be the safety of her motel room.

For the first time since she moved to Devils Point she kind of dreaded returning to an empty hotel room alone.

Not alone, she reminded herself.

Somewhere in these woods she was surrounded by pack. They were out there to make sure she got home safe tonight, as well as apprehend anyone who might follow. But where was the rogue? They'd zeroed in on one of her show admirers who wasn't one of her regulars as the likely guy, because his interest in her seemed intense.

He didn't try to touch or talk to her like many of them did. He just sat there staring with a weird look on his face...

This wasn't helping. Her imagination was headed for crazy town and each step she took felt slower than the last, making her want to run. Maybe she should, her thoughts taunted. Dante hated the plan from the get go, describing it as too dangerous. If she wanted to bail he would gladly come up with another idea.

What good would it do her sister if they captured the stupid wolf after he bit her or worse? Her newly wolfed out sister might kick her ass just for good measure.

Thinking of Faith and the reason she was doing this to begin with, eased a little of the tightness currently constricting her chest. But not by much.

Her mind still raced and her heart felt like it wanted to beat right out of her chest. Her head too. It didn't feel right. There was something slowing her brain down. A fog. It was harder to think than it should be.

She just had to get a little bit farther and she'd be out in the open. She could practically taste her freedom. Rebel paused. Hold on. Being out in the open meant their plan had failed. No cover, no wolf. If he was going to make a move he would do it before she made it out of the woods. That's what the pack had said.

She glanced behind her and squinted to see into the darkness. Maybe she should take a little more time and circle the trail, make it seem like she was going on a walk.

No. No. No. Her mind screamed. Go home. Get away.

Not paying full attention to where she put her feet, Rebel tripped and fell to her knees, slamming on a rock that tore into her flesh.

"Damn it," she cried.

Then she heard it again. Another twig crunched as if under someone's foot. She *was* being followed. Her mind raced, looking for an escape. Was she supposed to wait or run?

Logical thought fled and irrational thoughts prevailed. *Must run now.*

Blindly, she reached for the purse she dropped when she fell and began running down the trail. Time was up and she didn't care if the plan didn't work. She tried to pull more air into her lungs and failed. Screw this. She couldn't breathe. She couldn't think. It was time to pull herself together. Still her legs pumped harder and after a few seconds of blindness, she could see the break in the trees up ahead.

She was almost there.

The hairs on her neck were on high alert again and she swore it felt like someone was breathing on the back of her neck.

Don't look back.

Don't do it.

Do. *Not.* Look. Back.

She had to keep saying the words or she was going to do something dumb like look back and fall again, this time breaking her neck or worse, falling prey.

Moving faster than before, she burst through the trees out into the open and slammed straight into something hard.

Whoosh. The air burst from her lungs and she started to fall backwards. Except she didn't. Something stopped her.

"Rebel." A voice she couldn't fully make out through the fog filling her brain said her name. Someone had caught her and was holding her tightly in their arms, keeping her captive. Oh God. Panic tore through as she struggled, barely able to move an inch. Too tight. He was holding her too tight. And it was so dark, she couldn't see a thing.

This was it.

"Damn it, Rebel. Open your eyes and look at me." The thread of steel laced into the man's voice wiggled through her thoughts, making her want to obey more than hide.

She glanced up and cracked her eyes into very small slits.

"Dante?" she asked, more confused than sane.

"Yes, everything is fine, baby. You can take a breath now, I've got you." His hands stroked her back, soothing her.

She still couldn't catch her breath and her chest hurt more than ever, but his touch went a long way to making her feel a little better. "Not okay," she whispered.

"Tell me. What spooked you?"

She shook her head frantically back and forth. "Not spooked."

"Uh huh. Even without my exceptional hearing, I can hear your heart beating a mile a minute, babe. You are definitely freaked out. Tell me what happened. Did we miss something? No one saw a thing."

Rebel couldn't speak because she couldn't catch her breath. Her head grew lighter and her stomach roiled. This was not going well at all.

"You're freaking me out," Dante said just as someone else broke through the brush behind them.

Rebel didn't look to see who it was, her mind instead going into full blown panic mode, and letting loose with a scream guaranteed to be louder than a banshee calling for its mate.

FOUR

Dante fought the struggling woman in his arms, surprised at how strong she was when he couldn't easily contain her. At least not without hurting her. This was crazy. He and Diego were the closest to her and neither of them had seen anything unusual.

"What happened?" Damien came running up behind them. "Did he show up?"

He shook his head. "Not sure. She started panicking not long after she left the club. I had to intercept her before she freaked out."

Dante ignored his brother's further questions and whispered into Rebel's ear. "Shhh, baby. It's okay. You're safe with me. Nothing is going to happen to you."

But was that true? His heart was beating as fast as hers and he needed to get it under control before something happened that shouldn't.

He'd scented her fear almost immediately when she came out of the club. It was so strong it assaulted him every bit as much as it did her. So much so the need to protect her pushed at him in every direction until he could fight it no longer. By the time he got to her, she was in a full out run and scared out of her mind. Her panic had become his and the only thing keeping him human and together was the way she clung to him for support.

He had to soothe his mate.

The word ricocheted through his brain before he could stop it. Except she wasn't. At least not in the way of Dante and Faith being fated true mates. Despite his overpowering desire to protect her, he'd sensed no mate bond between them. Dante shook his head. Fuck it all. The rub of trying to let go of Rebel to find something all mighty powerful was pissing him off.

He wanted her. Only her. She got to him in so many ways and even in her panic she aroused him. He wanted her. It was that simple.

Fuck fate.

The more she squirmed against him the harder he got. Only it wasn't just his body that ached for her. Not when he couldn't get her out of his brain either. Yes, mating season made lust stronger. Hell, it made everything stronger. Including his growing feelings for the woman now trembling against him. The idea that someone else could come along and pull him away from her because of some destined fate made him angry beyond words.

"C'mon, let's get you home." He scooped her into his arms and she burrowed her face in his shoulder not saying a word. When they got to his truck and he slid her into the passenger seat she finally seemed to realize where they were and where he wasn't taking her.

"I thought you were taking me home. The motel is right there." She pointed to the building just down the hill as if I didn't know exactly where she lived. It was a decent place, but she deserved more.

"I am. To my home."

She blinked, uncertainty filling her gaze. "What? Why?"

"Because that's where you belong." He didn't wait for her expected argument and instead closed her door and rounded the front of the truck to the driver's side. He was in no mood to argue. Between her fear and the wolf whining in his head, he'd had enough for one night.

By the time he opened his door, her trembling had stopped and there was fire in her eyes. He smiled, satisfied he'd distracted her. He much preferred her like this, even if it did mean there would probably be a fight in his near future.

"Don't you smile at me like some stupid cat with a stupid secret," she said, sarcasm dripping off of each syllable.

"Wolf, remember? We don't do cats."

She sat back in her seat and crossed her arms. "As if I could forget."

He climbed in and fastened his seatbelt, taking his time to fish the keys out of his pocket and stick them into the ignition. If she wanted to stew over what he'd said, fine by him. As long as she realized he wasn't taking no for an answer. Tonight, it was his way or--his way.

They'd used her as bait tonight. And even though it didn't seem to work, they'd gotten close. The barely there scent of the strange wolf lingered on the air near where she'd burst out of the woods. He had to have figured out something was up. Either from the sheer panic attack that gripped Rebel almost from the second she emerged from the club or from the scent of his pack. It wasn't easy hiding your scent from another wolf. When it came to smell, hearing and sight they were on a pretty level playing field.

With a sideways glance at Rebel, he turned over the engine and backed out of his parking spot as he waited for the coming explosion. If ever there was a woman who didn't like doing as she's told it was definitely her.

"I don't know if me going to your place is a good idea." She finally said. "I don't even know where you live."

"The island's not that big. It wouldn't be hard to figure out if you really wanted to." He kept glancing over at her, shocked that she wasn't yelling at him yet.

"It's big enough," she said. "The island I mean. It's not so small I feel claustrophobic, but small enough that you pretty much know everyone who lives here. I like that."

He stared at her. That had to be the most information he'd heard from her at one time about why she liked living here. That she felt this comfortable around the pack had to mean something.

"I like it too. Not everyone here is pack, but everyone here is part of our family in one way or another."

"I'm part of your family?" She sounded like she didn't believe a word he said.

"Of course you are. Your sister is my brother's mate. That makes you family through and through."

Her shoulders sagged at his answer and he puzzled over her new frown. "Of course," she said. "Because of faith."

If it wasn't for the wolf DNA I would not have heard the last. As it was, though, he could and he did.

"You don't want to be family?" His instincts told him to tread carefully. Her resentment had been clear, and Rebel didn't like being pressed for personal information.

"I don't know what I want. Well, I wanted to catch that jerk of a werewolf tonight so we wouldn't have to go through that again, but I pretty much screwed that up. Now I don't know what to do next."

He didn't like the sound of that. "Don't sweat it. We won't be doing that again." He'd make sure of that. "It was a long shot to begin with. Rogue or not, weres have instincts humans don't. It's how we've stayed secret so long. As long as we're careful that can continue to be the case."

"How long? How did this even happen? Did someone get bitten and it just spread?"

Dante shrugged at her rapid fire questions that had no real answers. "There's a lot of hearsay and stories about how we were created and where it all started, but no one is sure anymore. Some say we're magical and created from an ancient race and others say we came about from some sort of freak experimentation gone wrong. The stories are so convoluted now no one knows the truth anymore."

"That sucks. If I was able to shift into a wolf I'd like to know why."

He sighed. "My brothers and I were born as shifters. It is all we've ever known and we like it." It may sound weird to you, but it's our nature. And it really can be fun."

She smiled softly at him. "Pack through and through."

"Something like that." He turned down his drive and wound his truck through the dense vegetation, and under a canopy of trees until it opened up into a clearing in front of his house. There was no need for outside lights since he could see perfectly in the dark, but thanks to the full moon his home was bathed in a soft glow of light, giving her quite the view.

"Wow. I didn't even know there was a house back here."

"Exactly. We designed it like that," he said. "We like our privacy and this place ensures it. The few tourists and strangers we get on the island won't wander back here. And the pack knows to call first before showing up."

He used the remote clipped to his visor to open the garage door and pulled the truck fully inside before setting it to close behind him. Before he could hop down and get to the passenger door, Rebel was already out her door and wandering through his yard.

When he caught up with her she turned back to him and asked, "We? You don't live here alone?"

H e nodded. "I share this house with Diego and while I said the pack calls first, the exception to that is after a hunt. Everyone likes to come out here and decompress. Besides, it's mating season and those of us not paired up need the distraction."

Rebel scrunched up her beautiful face. "Are you saying the entire pack is going to be here tonight because we were hunting that asshole?"

Dante nodded. That's exactly what he meant. Judging from the myriad of scents lingering out front, many were already here and it wouldn't be long before the rest arrived and it turned into a full-fledged party. "I'd offer to take you back to your room if you prefer, but you're not safe there right now. I scented the rogue outside the club, but there was something wrong with the scent and I can't put my finger on it. Until I figure it out we stick together. Okay?"

While she looked like she wanted to say something more, she seemed to think twice about it and simply nodded.

He opened the door and ushered her into the mudroom where they discarded their jackets and shoes. The scents of his family and raw meat filled the air. His stomach grumbled. If he couldn't get one hunger slaked he might as well feed the other.

They also had the fire pit going and music playing inside and out. It was gearing up to be a free for all.

Dante led Rebel up the stairs that opened into the wide-open space they used for a combination kitchen, living room and casual dining room. Three of the four walls were nothing but windows that during the daytime, and at night for him, provided a view as far as the eye could see.

Rebel looked around in open wonder. "Holy crap. I love these windows. It makes me feel like I'm up in a treehouse."

He smiled. There was nothing more that he loved than being surrounded by nature and his home was no exception. The solid walls of windows kept him connected to the outdoors day and night. He got the best of both worlds. The conveniences that made human life pleasant, with the beauty of nature that soothed the wolf inside.

"I can't take credit for much of this place. The design was all Diego's. He is a master carpenter with striking vision. I just get to enjoy it."

"Thanks, bro. Even though you did complain through the whole project."

Diego walked up behind them while they stood staring out the windows. He turned to Rebel. "Glad to see you're feeling better."

A bright red flush crawled up her neck and into her cheeks as she turned away from them. "I'm sorry I screwed up. I know how important it was to lure that jerk in tonight. I'm not sure what got into me."

Dante squeezed her arm and pulled her against his side. "Don't be sorry," he said with a smile. "We're all just glad you're safe." He brushed his lips across her hair, sending a fresh wave of heat coursing through his body. There was so much about her that I couldn't get enough of.

Diego pinched his brows and stared at him for a few seconds, before speaking. "He's right. Using you as bait was too dangerous. We shouldn't have done that." He rubbed his belly and smiled. "I don't know about you two, but I'm starving. I'm going to go check and see if we're ready to get the steaks and ribs on the grill yet."

Diego shot him a parting look full of warning that Dante intended to ignore. As far as he was concerned his brother could mind his own business.

Rebel glanced around the room looking a little like a rabbit about to take off. "You've got a lot of people here tonight."

Dante pulled her toward the open glass doors and out onto the balcony. "Just take a deep breath. Let the fresh air soothe you. You're in paradise and among friends. And there's no safer place on the island."

"That woo woo earth crunchy stuff doesn't exactly work on me. I'm not like you, remember?"

And thank God for that. If she was like him they probably wouldn't even be out here right now and his body wouldn't be rock hard as he maneuvered her into a dark corner.

"Nature has a way of putting everyone's troubles in perspective if you let it. That's nature not woo woo." He brushed the bright red hair from the side of her face, across a few scattered freckles on her skin, and trailed his fingers down to her jaw. She shivered under his touch, goose bumps rising on her perfect ivory skin. He wasn't surprised to find her affected as well. They'd already discovered their desire for each other after a couple of nights of heavy petting.

No, the initial attraction was not their problem. Nor was the lust pulsing through his blood.

Except now he wanted so much more. He ached for her. And didn't want to let her go. To the point he was entertaining ideas of being inside her right now. Her underneath him on the balcony floor, in his bed, on the kitchen island, and the list went on.

She looked up at him and licked her lips. The slight move of her moist tongue peeking out for a moment almost too much for him to bear. Shit. He needed a distraction now before he took this too far. Preferably with more people around.

"You want something to drink?"

She nodded, but her eyes spoke volumes more.

"Come." He grabbed her hand and led her to the kitchen, where half the pack was congregated. Some preparing pots of beans and bowls of salad to go with the meat, and others lining up shots of tequila.

"Dante! Rebel! Finally!" They were immediately enveloped in a round of hugs for her and generous pats on the back for him. Along with a repeated chorus of "We'll get him next time" from the not so sober crowd. Which meant many of them had to have been drinking for a while, and some were just getting started. Not that he minded. Between mating season and the two new strangers they were dealing with, the pack had to be feeling the stress.

They deserved a break, and an opportunity to cut loose without the pressure of mating season for at least a few hours.

"You two ready to join us in a round of shots? You've got some catching up to do." Everyone laughed and a round of cheers erupted among them.

He laughed. It felt great to see everyone in such good cheer. But he had something else on his mind. "Nah, maybe later. I promised Diego I'd man the grill tonight and for the sake of good food, I'll hold off on the tequila."

"Awwwww." Several of the group mock whined.

"I'll do some." Rebel spoke up and all eyes turned to her.

There were a few heartbeats of silence before Creed, one of the pack enforcers stepped forward. "Well, all right then. Let's do it."

One of the other guys grabbed another shot glass out of the cabinet and filled it before handing it to Rebel. "Salt is in the container behind you and the limes are in the bowl."

Amidst more hoots and hollering, everyone began licking the salt off their fingers and downing their tequila. This went on for a while as Dante prepared his — now famous among area packs — rib sauce and got everything ready for the grill all while keeping an eye on Rebel.

She already knew half the pack and she was easily holding her own with them. To his relief, there also seemed to be no remaining after effects of her earlier panic attack. Seeing her with that look of fear in her eyes had really gotten to him. He was prepared to do anything not to see it again. Bringing her had been a smart move on his part. In fact, it felt very comfortable having her in his home with all of his family and friends.

Unfortunately, this only seemed to deepen his need for her as the desire, not exactly cooled, flared to life every time he caught her scent or looked at her or heard her voice. And when she smiled at him...

As Diego would say, it was reaching epic proportions. Although why it was so strong without the pull of a potential true mate bond he didn't understand. He'd desired many women in his life and not once had one pulled at him this hard—even during mating season.

He glanced outside at the full moon and cursed. He felt betrayed by biology.

Not that it mattered anymore. He'd known from the moment she sacrificed herself to capture the man responsible for taking away her sister's choice that Rebel Harris would be his. And not just for this long ass mating season that felt like it was never going to end.

It was time to rock her world.

SIX

Rebel smiled at the joke Creed and Sawyer were regaling her with all while keeping an eye on Dante in her peripheral vision. Mostly, she watched him move since he was working side by side with Diego on the grill.

Every move he made some muscle or another flexed until she became mesmerized by the dance. She'd seen him naked more than once thanks to the shifter thing and he had an incredible body. Tight. So damn tight, especially his rock solid abs with their dips and ridges. What she wouldn't give right now to be touching him.

With her tongue.

Yes, the alcohol had gotten to her, but Dante had gotten to her a long time ago. And she still needed to get him out of her system. One slow lick at a time.

She tried to shake the thoughts from her head with no success. Once the image of her tongue touching that beautiful body hit her brain, it imprinted into her permanent memory.

"Hey, we're going to go get some more beer from the icebox downstairs. You want some?"

She forced her thoughts to Sawyer who had asked her a question. "Uhh...No I'm good."

"Okay. There's water in the fridge if you just want that."

She nodded at them both as they headed down the stairs before turning her full attention back to Dante who stood alone at the grill.

Now was her chance.

Her earlier conversation with Melody kept replaying in her head. They needed to have sex and just get it out of their system. She was convinced it was the only way to move on. She definitely didn't need to spend any more time on wondering what if when it came to climbing into bed with him.

It would just be sex. Easy peasy.

She moved closer to the patio door until she was just a few feet away from his back. This close she noticed a small trickle of sweat sliding down the side of his face. It would be so easy to lick that for him...

Rebel stifled a giggle. Yeah, she was pretty tipsy. But not so much she didn't know exactly what she was doing or what she wanted.

"Hey," she said.

Dante turned to the side and smiled at her. He looked so genuinely happy to see her she almost melted on the spot.

"There you are. Enjoying yourself?"

"I think we should have sex. Preferably as soon as possible," she blurted.

She didn't so much see his body go stiff as she felt all the oxygen get suddenly sucked up around them as he stared down at her. She held her breath waiting for him to say or do something.

It was then she noticed that all of the party noise had ceased and all heads and eyes were turned in her direction.

"I...uhh... I guess they all heard that, huh?"

Dante set down his cooking tools and grabbed her waist, pushing her back against the glass. Either he wasn't paying attention or he didn't care if everyone saw him.

He buried his face in her hair and breathed deep before he spoke. "This is not the time to joke about something like that, Rebel. You know it's mating season and we've got sex on the brain. A lot of sex."

"I wasn't joking," she whispered. "I am dead serious."

"Then you should feel exactly how serious I am." He leaned his hips forward and pressed the rigid length of his erection into her soft belly.

"Ohhh." She sighed. "Then my suggestion is not out of the question?"

"Definitely not. Especially when you smell this good."

Heat flashed through her. Both from arousal and a little embarrassment. It was going to take her a while to get used to the fact that werewolves could see, hear and especially smell better than she could. In fact, she was pretty sure he was referring to the fact her panties were wet with her desire.

"Can we do it tonight?" she asked.

He growled. Long and low, making the sound vibrate against her skin. Oh God, she liked that.

"We can go right now."

Something about the urgency in his voice snapped her back to awareness. "Is everyone watching us right now?"

He lifted his head and looked over her shoulder. "Yep."

"Shit. And can they smell—"

"Probably. You smell fertile."

Her head jerked back. "I smell what? Ewww." She wriggled free from his hold, probably because he let her and scooted away from him to the balcony railing. "Jesus, Dante. Did you really just say that? Do you have any clue how unsexy that is?"

"Maybe. But it's fucking delicious to wolves."

Her stomach fluttered at the guttural sound of his voice. The words didn't even really matter that much. Not when he pinned her with a stare that promised carnal delights she imagined out of her world and the vibrations in his voice hummed between her thighs. It was unusual to sense so much need from a man. Her body shook in response. She wasn't sure if her legs could hold her upright much longer at this rate.

"I think I'd rather do this without an audience. We could go back to my place."

He stalked forward. His eyes tinged with yellow at the edges. His wolf close to the surface. At least that's how Faith explained it when her eyes did that.

"Are you going to shift?"

"No. But the wolf inside is powerful and he has needs right now too. Mating season is not easy on either of us."

"You talk about your wolf like it's a second person. Why?" She was stalling and they both knew it.

"Because it's easier for non shifters to grasp when I do. The wolf is a part of me, but he's not all of me. I'm human too. The best of both worlds actually."

"Top of the food chain." It wasn't a question and he didn't answer.

He placed his hands on the rail behind her, one on each side of her, trapping her. "What are we going to do now? Don't you have to finish cooking those ribs?"

"They'll keep."

"Until when?"

"Until after I kiss you." He no sooner said the words and his mouth came down on hers. The heat of his lips shocked her, enough that she parted her lips and his tongue slid inside. With a combination of hard pressure and delightful licks he plunged forward, exploring every inch of her.

Her head nearly exploded. Her chest constricted and blood rushed through her ears. She grabbed onto the collar of his shirt and pulled him closer until they were leaning halfway across the railing with his chest pressing down on her aching breasts. Heat coiled in her belly moments before it sprang forward and out to her arms and legs.

There was no house, no pack, no stars and no sky. There was only Dante touching her and sending shock waves through her system like little tendrils looking for a place to take hold and grow.

What was happening to her? It was just a kiss.

Her toes tingled and scalp prickled from his fingers tugging at the thick strands of her hair. She didn't know how to explain it anymore.

When the crowd in the house started howling and cheering, they broke apart gasping for breath. Well, more like she jumped away from him and he slowly eased away as if not affected in the least. She gulped for air while he leaned against the deck railing looking ridiculously sexy.

"Bad timing, huh?" she asked.

"There is no bad time for you to tell me what you need."

Her stomach flipped. Good answer. She glanced over her shoulder at all the faces watching them through the windows. "I'll admit I've done some pretty crazy things in my life, but public sex isn't one of them. Maybe we could continue this discussion later after all your friends have gone home."

"On one condition." His mouth quirked to a half smile.

"Now I'm nervous." She licked her lips and waited.

A sexy rumble rolled from his chest. "You should be because some of the things I'd like to do to you might not be exactly legal in all fifty states."

Her body jerked in response and his eyes widened. He was too perceptive for his own good. "Is that a threat or a promise," she asked.

"Come here."

Feeling compelled to give this man anything he wanted, she stepped forward until he caught the hem of her shirt and pulled her the rest of the way. She smashed into his chest and braced her hands on tight pectorals to steady herself.

"Kiss me again," he demanded.

In the space of those three growled words she forgot about everyone else in the house. Seeing only him and his hazel and gold eyes full of heat, she leaned forward and tentatively pressed her lips to his. From there he took control, biting down on her lower lip and sucking it into his mouth.

I'm going to pay for this later, a part of her mind whined. I'll never be the mate he wants.

When he let go of her now slightly swollen lip and his tongue swept inside her mouth, the rest of her stupid brain told her to shut up and go with the plan.

Rebel grabbed his shoulder and squeezed as her knees weakened. Because they were plastered together from chest to knees, his hard cock pressed to her abdomen. She was still shocked by how huge he was, but it was the fact he wanted her too that truly empowered her.

His hands went from her hips and moved up her sides until his fingers brushed the edges of her breasts.

"You're so damned beautiful, Rebel," he whispered against her lips. "I've been waiting for you."

Her heart hammered from his words as he kissed her again, then bent to her throat. Every spot his lips touched, her skin sizzled. Her breath quickened making it hard to breathe. His fingers continued to stroke along the sides of her breasts and then under the curve of the front. He was so damned hot and this was no ordinary kiss. It was possessive, broadcasting to every other shifter within a mile that she was marked as his.

It's what Damien did with Faith...

She pulled back, breaking the kiss and gulped for breath. "You're dangerous," she said, not sure whether she was talking to him or reminding herself.

"Why? Because I'm considering taking you right here on a balcony? Or because I'd do or say anything just to be inside you?"

Rebel stood there considering the situation and was about to throw caution to the wind when Dante's head jerked up. Before she could figure out what was happening she heard a pop and he dove for her, yanking her to the ground.

"Get down!" he yelled.

No sooner did the words come out of his mouth and the window behind her shattered into a million pieces and rained down on them. Her mouth opened to scream and Dante's hand roughly covered it.

"Stay quiet."

The lights inside the house suddenly winked out and they were enveloped in darkness. Dante moved his head and placed his lips right at her ear and whispered, "Follow my lead and don't make a sound. I'm going to get you out of here. Nod your head if you're good."

She nodded, her heart lodged in her throat as fear seized her.

He scooped her into his arms and keeping his back to the open balcony he half crawled half walked inside the house. It was so dark she couldn't see beyond a few inches in front of her. He could though.

Another shot rang out and Rebel flinched at the same time Dante stumbled. Fortunately he righted himself before they fell and he jumped forward. For a few seconds she couldn't breathe as they flew through the air until Dante landed with an oomph. His grip tightened and he ran downward.

Or at least she thought that was happening. It was hard to tell in her disoriented state in the darkness. Still, she was afraid to speak and bit her lip to keep quiet.

Seconds later Dante banged something in front of them and then behind them. A moment later bright light flooded the room and she squinted against the harsh glare.

"We're safe. Are you okay?" He set her down on her feet and started touching her. "Are you hit?" he asked.

"I'm fine. But what the hell is going on?"

"Someone's shooting at us. You're sure you're not hit?"

She pushed his hands away. "I'm fine. Seriously? But where is everyone else?"

"Hunting and I've got to join them."

"What? No way, you can't go out there."

"I can and I am. Don't worry you'll be safe here." He started easing away from her.

"But what about you? It's not safe for you out there either. Even a wolf can't escape a bullet."

"You'll be safe here. Just stay put and I'll be back for you as soon as it's safe. The pack needs my help."

Tears were filling her eyes. The thought of Dante going out there to hunt someone with a gun in the dark was more than she could handle. "Please, Dante. Don't go out there."

"I have to. You'll be safe here," he repeated.

"Stop saying that," she cried. "Just take me with you."

"No."

The growled word left no room for argument. Plus he moved so damned fast she barely saw it. One minute he was standing in front of her and she was clinging to him to keep him safe and the next minute he was gone.

Anger and fear washed over her as she looked around the room. What the hell was she supposed to do alone in this stupid windowless room?

That was when she looked down and found her shirt soaked with blood...

Dante tore through the woods behind his house, ripping the bloody shirt off as he ran. Anger fueled him as he followed the scent of his pack. They were in pursuit and he planned to find them before they caught their prey. It shook him to his core that Rebel could have been killed tonight. Another inch or two and that bullet would have struck her heart instead of him.

He wanted to shift to catch up quicker, but a part of him needed to stay like this to keep control of the instinct to kill that hammered through him. If the wolf took over now he wasn't sure he could stop himself from killing the culprit. They might seem more human than not, but when it came to certain things like protecting a mate they were pure animal instinct.

In the darkness he saw nothing, but not far ahead a wolf howled and he ran harder. His brother was moving in on the shooter. With nowhere for his eyes to focus on, he continued to scan while focusing on speed. The rest of the pack had to be close. Even if they split up, Dante would not be alone.

He burst through the trees and into the clearing on the opposite side of the island and nearly crashed into Diego.

"Where is he?" he snarled.

Two others already shifted rushed in from opposite sides, looking as confused as him.

Diego growled. "I can still smell him but I can't tell in which direction."

Dante stuck his nose in the air and took in and catalogued every scent he recognized, searching for the one he didn't. The salt in the air, the sand beneath his feet, and the pack filtering through the trees. There was only one other and it was faint. A barely there mint that led down the beach.

"This way." He turned to run and Diego caught his arm.

"You're shot."

"I'll live. That's more than I can say for the bastard who shot at my mate."

"Whoa. Whoa. Whoa. I thought we talked about this?"

Dante wrenched his arm free from his brother. "I'm done talking about it. What I feel for her isn't going away just because she isn't a true mate. Now I'm going to kill the person who tried to take her away from me and you're either with me or you're not. Your choice."

A wide smile crossed Diego's face. "About fucking time."

Dante's body jerked. "What?"

"That means I'm with you." He said nothing more before his bones began to pop and he flowed into a strong brown wolf. He yipped, telling Dante to get on with it.

He smiled and followed suit, ignoring the pain from the gunshot wound and the crack of his bones as he let the wolf have some freedom. With the pack by his side, some of the rage making him lose control subsided. If only temporarily.

Together, they bounded down the beach hard and fast as the scent of mint grew stronger. A loud bang sounded and they both hit the ground as a bullet whizzed by them, so close Dante felt the hair on his back part from the force.

Shit.

He stayed low and moved into the brush. His prey was close. He and Diego split up and soundlessly moved in on the shooter. The scent of mint was so strong it nearly gagged him.

His blood thirst rose, the sound of a gun cocking the only thing he heard.

Dante opened his senses and allowed the wolf to take the reins. His hearing sharpened and the sudden sound of the hunter breathing slow and steady filled his ears. He controlled his breathing, but not the racing of his heartbeat or the extra flow of adrenalin making his blood rush through his veins.

Judging by what he heard, the gunman trying to kill him or his mate stood only a few yards away behind one of the nearby trees.

Time to flush this fucker out.

He half growled and half snarled, amping up the volume, making sure his pack heard his claim.

He's mine, it said.

The pulse of his prey sped up. His fight or flight instinct kicked in and the barrel of the rifle came around the tree, firing off a shot a second before he ran. Dante's own adrenalin spiked and he jumped from the rock he'd climbed on for a better vantage point. A howl broke the night air from in front of the hunter and he stumbled and scrambled back to his feet just in time for Dante to land on his back and take him to the ground, the air whooshing from both their lungs.

The wolf didn't hesitate to wrap his mouth around the man's neck and clamp down with his teeth.

"No!!"

Through the din of his own blood rushing in his ears, Dante heard his brother screaming at him as he ran into the clearing naked and in human form once again. "You can't kill him. We need answers."

Fuck that. Dante snarled without releasing the human.

"Diego's right." Damien entered the fray, approaching him both quickly and cautiously.

Dante tried to fight the kill instinct, but its talons we're embedded so deep into his psyche he couldn't shake it.

"Rebel is safe, remember? Locked in the safe room. We have time to get answers before we dispatch this fucker."

Mate.

"That's right. You need to get back to her. Show her you're all right. She's waiting for you, big guy."

Damien and Diego were both now touching his neck, lending him their strength and soothing the wolf. Dante finally felt the wolf recede as he conceded to his brothers' wishes. His mouth released the human's neck and licked the drop of blood from his tooth not at all appeased but willing to give them a little time.

But only a little.

He jumped off the hunter's back and flowed back to his human body, his muscles coiled tight and ready to attack at the first opportunity.

"All right asshole. If you have any desire to stay alive you better start talking." Diego grabbed the hunter's shoulder and jerked him around so he was on his back and yanked off the idiot's hat that obscured his face.

Holy shit.

All three of them took a step back. Their gunman wasn't a man at all. What they saw was so fucked up they were all too shocked to speak.

Lying on the ground at their feet was a blonde haired, blue-eyed bombshell dressed in flannel and shit kickers, with a handgun aimed squarely between Dante's eyes.

"Get your filthy hands off me," she spat in Diego's direction without taking her eyes from her new target.

"Unless you want me to hand you over to him," Damien pointed to Dante, "I'd suggest you put your gun down and try some manners. You are not only trespassing, but you shot my brother tonight and could have hurt our women. So we are not in a forgiving mood."

"I could care less about your mood," she said. "Your pack hurt my brother. I'll shoot every one of you if I have to."

Dante growled, "Unlike you, we don't go around hurting people unless they've done something to deserve it. Who the hell is your brother and what did we supposedly do to him exactly?"

"One of you bastards bit him. Now I'm supposed to find him and put him down." Her gun faltered for a split second at the last of her statement. Clearly, she was distressed about what she'd come for.

"Why would your people make you come here and do this? Do they not watch out for their women?" This time Diego asked the questions. He had a strange look on his face that Dante couldn't read.

"We don't coddle women where I come from. I sure as hell don't need some man to do my hard jobs. I'm perfectly capable."

Still staring at her gun, Dante responded. "I can see that. However, I don't know where you got your information but it's wrong. No one in our pack would bite a human unless it was an accident or they were forced to defend themselves. Besides, that's something we would have heard about."

"Sounds like high and mighty bullshit to me. My brother was tracking wolves in this area when he went missing. Then he called me a couple of weeks ago and said he was bitten. Took me that long to track him here, but make no mistake, he's here and someone here will be held accountable."

Dante was getting tired of listening to her excuses. He had an overdose of energy with nowhere to go at the moment and the pain of getting shot was starting to get past the extra adrenalin. Not to mention he was getting antsy to get back to Rebel. He was going to have one angry female on his hands.

Thinking of getting back home to his mate distracted him and he didn't realize how woozy he felt until he swayed forward and Damien had to catch him.

"Whoa, big boy. You can't pass out now. That little gun of hers may be tiny but it'll pack a hell of a punch."

"Already got one hole in me. Don't need another."

"No, you certainly don't." He turned to the woman still trying to threaten them. "You'll hand over your guns to Diego and go with him now. You are outmatched by an entire pack." As if on cue, the rest of the pack emerged from the trees and filled the small clearing.

Her eyes widened, but she didn't immediately lower her gun. "Who's to say I put down my gun and you don't kill me right here, right now?"

"Me," Dante said. "If a human is bitten we need to look into it. That alone buys you a little time." He paused. "But only a little."

She thought about it for a few more seconds and then flipped her gun handle out and Diego scooped it up. He released the clip and threw it into the bay, followed by the gun in a different direction.

"Hey!" she yelled.

"We don't need guns on our island." Diego grabbed her arm and hauled her to her feet. "Let's go." He turned back to Dante. "Go get your woman out of our basement. I think I'm going to need it."

EIGHT

Rebel paced from one end of the room to the other. She had no idea how long she'd been cooped up in this room since there wasn't a damn clock on the wall and her cell phone was upstairs in her purse. Although it might as well have been days as angry as she was.

What if Dante was dead?

The thought made her blood run cold.

He better be all right or she was going to kill him. She rubbed her arms as if that would help wipe away some of the worry. Nothing helped. What could be taking so long?

She turned and walked in the opposite direction, surprised there wasn't already a traffic pattern worn in the carpet.

A click at the door had Rebel going on alert. There was nothing in the room to use as a weapon, she'd already checked, so she sure hoped it was Dante coming in and not some stranger.

She volunteered for this wild plan of her own free will, but that didn't mean she wanted to die tonight at the hands of some crazy soaked hunter willing to shoot down anyone that got in his way.

The door flung open and Dante appeared in the doorway, clad only in a pair of jeans and caked dried blood streaking down his arm and chest.

"Oh thank God." She rushed forward and gently grabbed his injured arm. "Are you okay? I've been frantic. I didn't realize there was blood until after you'd gone.

"I'll be fine. Not the first time I've been shot."

Rebel ignored that. She most certainly did not want to entertain the idea this kind of thing happened all the time for him. She also refrained from screaming and punching at him for locking her in this room. For now.

"Did someone call nine-one-one? We need to get you to a hospital."

"Really, it's not that big of a deal." His voice came out strong despite the unusually pale color of his skin and haunted look in his eyes.

"Well, we have to do something. You're not going to heal with your skin hanging open like that. At the very least you need some stitches." She leaned over and inspected the mangled wound a little closer. "Oh for Christ's sake. There's a bullet still lodged in there."

He nodded. "That explains why it's not healed yet."

She grabbed his hand and started pulling him toward the door. "Well, C'mon then. If we can't take you to the hospital then I'm going to at least pull that slug out of you and stitch you closed."

His eyes widened. "You know how to do these things?"

She shrugged. "I've never pulled a bullet out, but I'm damned good with a pair of tweezers and a sewing kit which, unless you've got a doctor in your pocket, is better than nothing."

"I don't have a sewing kit here," he said, stopping them both in their tracks.

She turned back to him. "Then good thing I'm here. I have a fully stocked purse for every kind of wardrobe malfunction right up those stairs."

He pulled his eyebrows together. "What the hell is a wardrobe malfunction and what does that have to do with getting a bullet out?"

Rebel started laughing, so hard she doubled over. "You should see your face right now. Oh my God. Priceless.

Forget about the wardrobe and just trust me. I got this."

He looked down at his bare torso and she followed his line of sight. Yes, she'd noticed the rippling abs, perfectly formed pecs and the mouthwatering trail of hair that led below the waistband of his jeans. Under different circumstances she probably would've already tried following it. The mere thought of getting inside his pants and investigating made her wet. Talk about inconvenient.

As she tried to bank the building heat inside her, Dante's head shot up and his nostrils flared.

"You're aroused," he said.

Oh crap.

"You are, I can scent it." A slightly amused smile crossed his face.

"GD shifter senses. I am not aroused, I'm irritated. Let's go." She tried to pull him out of the room and he stayed rooted to the spot.

"You can't lie to me." He stared at her, looking deep.

She tried to out stare him but the man was tenacious beyond belief obviously oblivious to the pain in his arm. "Fine," she said. "But it doesn't matter because I wasn't lying about being irritated. Although make that pissed. You locked me in a basement."

"For your own good. And I'll do it again if I have to. I won't let anyone hurt what's mine."

"The fact you aren't a little sorry for scaring the living hell out of me just pisses me off more. Now, let's go before I change my mind about helping you." She ignored the little tidbit about "mine." She chalked it up to the adrenalin talking.

This time when she pulled his hand, he followed.

"Better scared than dead, yes?"

How was she supposed to argue that logic? "Then the least you can do is install a stupid phone down there or something. And a clock!" She shook her head. Why on earth did she want to stay on this island? That was the million dollar question wasn't it? And the question she already knew the answer to despite his pig headed behavior.

She was in love with a wolf.

Rebel stood back and admired her handiwork. "Not bad if I say so myself. And almost a painless process."

"Speak for yourself. You digging in there with your pink glittery tweezers was no hunt on a full moon. It hurt like hell."

She frowned. "Why didn't you say something? I would have tried to be more gentle."

He grabbed her around the waist and pulled her between his legs where he sat on a stool. "No need. It had to come out and now that it has, I'll heal a lot faster." His voice lowered. "I'm impressed you were willing to remove it in the first place."

"It was no hunt on a full moon, but I survived."

He threw back his head and laughed, a deep rumble she felt low in her belly.

"Already picking up the lingo. Does that mean you've decided to stay?"

She tried to pull away and he gripped her waist tighter.

"Don't leave me," he said.

"I—I can't stay and you know it." It was going to rip her in two to leave, but watching him try to be something he couldn't would hurt far worse. He deserved a bond like Faith and Damien and the only way that could happen was if she left.

"Then why were you trying to get me in bed earlier?"

Rebel winced. Why couldn't he have forgotten that part? So much had happened since that unfortunate moment out on the deck. Was it really still the same night? The way the sky was beginning to lighten outside his bank of windows, the night was over and so was her chance.

"We've both been up all night and you've got to be ready to crash. I know I am." Except her crash and burn was coming from a broken heart.

"Agreed. We both need sleep." He stood and scooped her into his arms.

"Dante, what are you doing?" She grabbed his shoulders to steady herself.

"Taking you to bed so you can sleep." He started walking up another set of stairs.

"That's not what I meant. I need to go back to my motel."

"No." He must have sensed her agitation because he softened his tone. "I'm tired, babe. You are too. I have a big bed and having you next to me will assist the healing process."

"Is that a shifter thing?"

He nudged a door at the top of the steps open and walked through it. "Mmmhmm." He set her down on the edge of a big very soft bed that looked a hundred times more inviting than her crappy motel bed. She was tired.

"Here." Dante handed her a shirt. "You can sleep in that so you'll be more comfortable. I'll replace the shirt I ruined tomorrow."

"That's not necessary. I will use this one though for the night. Thank you." She hurried to the bathroom and changed, tossing her shirt into his trash and folding her jeans and bra on the counter. The shirt said Deadman's Island with a skull and crossbones on it and it smelled like Dante, clean with a hint of musk and the outdoors. Maybe she'd tell him she wanted to keep it in exchange for her other one.

With a heavy sigh she returned to the bedroom and found Dante already in the bed. Thanks to the wall of windows in this room too, she could make him out clearly.

Bare except for his boxer briefs, she took a moment to admire all of his beautiful flesh. Clearly shifters were made from a different mold. One that included low body fat, thick muscles and a cock much bigger than normal men.

He had an arm thrown over his face and the steady rise and fall of his chest indicated he was already asleep. He'd been through hell tonight.

Diego let them know earlier that the hunter they captured had been secured and no one had anything more to worry about tonight. No sign of the rogue wolf. Although there was speculation that the wolf the hunter came looking for was the same as the one who bit her sister.

She yawned, turning her attention back to the big comfy bed with the beautiful man sleeping in it. Now would be the perfect time to leave. She could sneak out and be gone from the island long before he woke again.

"Stop thinking so hard, Rebel and get in the bed. We're both tired and I need you with me."

She groaned. Every time she thought about leaving he would say something sweet or intense that got to her. He said he needed her and that felt really good.

Unable to walk away from that feeling, she did as he said and climbed in next to him. Her body barely hit the mattress before his arms came out and snatched her to his side. "Need you, baby. Now go to sleep okay?"

"Okay," she said.

Dante hooked a leg over one of hers, pinning her underneath him.

"Rebel?"

"Mmmhmm?" His warmth and strong hold instantly made her feel drowsy.

"Please don't leave."

She smiled. "Dante?"

"Yeah?"

"Go to sleep."

He rumbled behind her and buried his face in her hair. "Okay, baby."

NINE

"Rebel." Someone shook her and she tried to hide under the pillow. It wasn't time to get up yet.

"Wake up, sleepy head."

In her sleep fogged brain she recognized Dante's voice.

"I think you should be awake for this," he growled.

Her eyes opened, squinting against the bright sunshine filling the room. "For what?"

"The first time I make love to you." His fingers were on her thighs and she was already imagining them sliding upward.

"What?"

He leaned forward and nuzzled her neck. "You heard me. I'm taking you up on your offer."

God that was so tempting. "We should talk about this. Last night there were extenuating circumstances. Now everything has changed."

"Bullshit. Last night you wanted to be with me and this morning you still do."

"You almost died last night. You were shot..." She glanced at his arm, shocked to see the skin had healed almost overnight. Other than a red line where she'd stitched him up he didn't even look injured.

He followed her gaze. "I told you shifters heal fast."

"There's fast and then there is ridiculous." She pushed at his shoulders and tried to squirm free. "This can't happen. I need to leave today."

"Damn it!" Dante growled. "Stop pushing me away. This is because of that true mate BS, isn't it?"

"It's not BS, you said so yourself. And look at Faith and Damien!" she yelled. "I've never seen two people so connected. It's—it's magical. So get off me because I can't do this. I will not be the one who stands by and watches you suffer because you didn't wait for the right one."

He grabbed her hands and lifted them over her head, pinning them down to the mattress. "Don't you get it?

You are the right one for me. I don't need a mystical bond to tell me that. I feel it every second of every day whether I am with you or not. Because all I can think about is you. Every fucking gorgeous inch of you that I need to taste, or your scent that refuses to leave my head. This is what being near you does to me."

He brought her hand between them and pressed it against the front of his body, making her feel his formidable erection. It was long and thick and warm and damn it, she wanted it.

"That's just lust," she fired back. "You'll get over it."

He lowered his head, his lips inches from hers. His eyes were changing from hazel to gold. "Is that what you really believed last night? We'd be together one time and then be over it? Well, you're wrong. For the rest of my life I will want to be with you. Inside of you. Around you. No one just gets over those kind of feelings. Not letting me claim you is killing me. Please, don't leave."

Please, don't leave.

She had no defense against that. Not when her heart already belonged to him. This whole situation was bigger than just the two of them. She was drawn to the island from the very beginning. Her love for dancing was a big fat lie she told herself as an excuse to stay longer than she should have.

Now she had the most beautiful, virile man on top of her and in her hands, pleading with her not to leave him. At what cost did he admit how much he needed her? Last night he could have died protecting her, reminding her how short life could be. If she left now could she even stop the pain of losing him or was it too late?

"Dante," she whispered.

He leaned down and pressed his lips softly against hers. "Please don't cry, baby." He wiped away the tears she didn't even realize were falling. "This is a good thing you and me. With or without the true mate thing, we'll be bonded. I'll belong to you heart and soul. Hell, I already do. Why else would I follow you around like a puppy?"

She laughed, her heart squeezing. "I like puppies almost as much as I like you."

Dante let out a groan. "Then it's settled. You'll stay."

It wasn't exactly a question, but she answered anyway. "Yes, Dante. I'll stay."

"Finally." Before she could respond his grip on her pinned wrist grew harder and his mouth came down on hers. This wasn't their first kiss and every one before it had been sublime, but this—this was different. This was intense.

He took her deeper with the stroke of his tongue while his free hand roamed her body. And he didn't just go for her breasts or pussy like most guys, he touched her everywhere, igniting heat as he went.

When she thought she might instantaneously combust or break apart from the force of her need, he pushed up her shirt and yanked down her underwear.

These were not the practiced moves of an experienced lover, this was hot and primal and it burned in her chest as much as everywhere else.

The cooler air of the room brushing her skin as he bared it did nothing to assuage the fire growing inside her. If anything it made it grow dangerously larger.

With her hand still pressed against his cock, she fumbled with the elastic of his shorts until she got him free. His size scared her a little, but she knew Dante would never hurt her.

As she wrapped her fingers around the rigid flesh he groaned into her mouth. "Can't wait," he mumbled, before using his legs to nudge her thighs open. He hooked his arm under one knee and lifted it high, effectively opening her wide. "Wrap your arm around my neck and hold on."

Her stomach tumbled at the order, making her eager to comply.

Looking down into her eyes he began pushing inside her. She dug her fingernails into his neck at the sensation of being spread open, her breath caught and her eyes widened.

"Relax, Rebel. I'm not going to hurt you."

"I know," she gasped. "It's just so—so..."

"Perfect," he groaned as he slid a little more inside.

Oh, God yes. It was so incredible she wanted to throw her head back and scream, but her body was trapped underneath his and it was all she could do to gasp for air.

Dante kissed her cheek. "Do you have any idea how beautiful you are?"

She pulled his head down and kissed him like he kissed her, pouring all of her emotions into that one touch. Dante hummed, sparking a series of vibrations as he pushed the rest of the way inside her. Fully seated, her body gripped him and instinct overrode coherent thought as she shuddered and adjusted.

He broke the kiss and buried his face in her neck, scraping her tender flesh with his sharp teeth. "To accept the bond means you'll likely turn. Are you sure you're ready for that?"

She looked up at him and nodded. Together they felt whole. She'd tried to fight it so he had a chance to live the life he needed, but she couldn't do it. Now she wanted to embrace it. It was so hard to imagine anyone else could love him more than she did when it consumed her like this.

When he didn't do anything she spoke. "Yes, I want to be with you. Whatever it takes."

Dante kissed her, his face so full of need she couldn't comprehend. She thought he was going to bite her, but instead he just kept kissing her as he rotated his hips, reminding her that being wrapped in Dante's heat with his cock buried inside her was the best damn thing she'd ever felt.

For months they'd danced around their need for each other only to bring them to this perfect moment that was about to change her world forever.

"Can I have my other hand?" she asked. "One is not enough. I need to touch everywhere."

Dante immediately released her pinned wrist and smiled down at her. "Anything for you, my lady."

She touched his face, tracing her finger across his lips and jaw. Her touch must have sparked something because he groaned and then moved, pulling his cock from her tight clasp. There was a brief moment where neither of them breathed before Dante slid back inside.

This time he didn't linger. Before she could take a breath, he withdrew again and immediately pushed forward. What he did to her body was nearly indescribable. Every drag across her sensitive tissues ignited explosions of sensation. He didn't stop there. His thrusts increased, as did the friction until there was nothing in her mind except Dante thick inside her and the heady joy of being with the man she loved.

Rebel moved with him, lifting to meet his hips on every downward stroke.

God it was beautiful. Friction and sweat and wildness.

"It's you. It has to be." His words came out hoarse. "I don't want to live in a world that doesn't include you. I love you. Have for a while now."

I love you too. She tried to say it but couldn't speak. She was too drunk on pleasure to form the words. Dante pumped, her body responded. It was all primal now. With the room bathed in sunshine at Dante's back and her arms and legs wrapped around him, the world disappeared and the room spun.

Dante moved his hips faster and faster as the sensation inside her coiled tight. He moved in a wild tempo that seemed to feed everything going on inside her. With his head thrown back as he pumped into her, she saw his eyes glowing bright and the sharpened points of his teeth poking into his lip.

The frenzy continued. Rebel couldn't move or breathe. She squeezed her eyes closed and rode the sensations until the binding holding her in broke and her world exploded. A scream tore from her throat, echoing the explosions in her head.

Dante somehow managed to slam into her one last time while sinking his teeth into the soft spot of her shoulder. The sudden burst of light flashing in her head drowned out everything as heat wrapped around her heart and squeezed.

When she finally was able to open her eyes, Dante was there waiting for her. Slick with sweat and his hands gliding across her skin. "Rebel," he groaned. He released the leg he still held and she wrapped it around his back. He was still inside her and she needed to stay like that for a while longer.

"Dante," she whispered.

"I know, baby. I know." Instead of saying more unnecessary words his mouth came down on hers in a savage kiss, one that said more than words ever could.

She imagined he did know how she felt right now. But there was something going on inside her she didn't understand and she wasn't sure if it had to do with her already becoming a wolf or something else. But they were connected and it wasn't simply by words of love. Those tendrils she felt yesterday had taken root and had given her what she wanted more than anything else.

A home. She was finally home...

The next day.

"So what happens now?" She reveled in the warmth of Dante's embrace as they languished in bed after another marathon session of how many ways can we have sex in one house.

The sun had yet to fully crest over the horizon, but the glow of it told her it was imminent.

It wasn't often she was awake at this time of day and she looked forward to enjoying the sunrise view from his treehouse bedroom. That's what she'd dubbed it the first time she'd seen it and that was how it would stay.

She had already fallen in love with everything about this house. Of course, the man had a lot to do with that. But it had been a long time since she'd had a real home, and while she was still afraid to fully say it out loud, everything about Dante felt like home.

"After breakfast we'll go to the motel and pack up your things and bring them back here."

"What?" She jackknifed into a sitting position faster than she thought possible.

"What?" He cracked an eye open and looked at her.

"I wasn't talking about us living together. I mean this." She pointed to the twin bite marks on her neck where he'd marked her. "Shouldn't something be happening by now?"

"Oh. That." He reached out and rubbed his fingers across them. He'd done that a lot since it had happened. It was an incredibly possessive move, and she couldn't help but love it.

"Don't get me wrong, it will be kind of nice not to live in a motel," she cautiously admitted. "But I think we have bigger concerns."

"All the more reason for you to stay here and as close to me as possible." He wrapped his arm around her waist and hauled her on top of him. "We wouldn't want you to go all wolfie on a tourist or something."

He nuzzled her neck with his nose and she groaned before tilting her head to the side to give him the access he wanted. That he proceeded to lick the spot where he'd bitten her probably shouldn't have felt almost as good as if he'd licked her between her legs, but there was no denying it. While nothing physical had seemed to change, there were changes.

Her skin was more sensitive for one. And when she looked out the window she seemed to see more than ever before. Or it could all be a figment of her imagination. She was both anxious and excited to see what being a wolf would feel like, but it seemed that she was getting ahead of herself.

Then a horrible thought struck her. "Oh my God. Am I going to have to worry about fleas?"

Dante barked out a laugh before he turned to her with a sober look. "I guess anything is possible."

Her stomach flipped and second thoughts flooded through her. She jumped up and paced back and forth across the room. "This is not good. There's like a potion or something I can take to prevent it, right? Please tell me that's a thing."

Dante's laughter returned and as he doubled over and grabbed his stomach, she realized he was messing with her.

"You jerk," she cried, picking up the nearest pillow and throwing it at his head. He caught it one handed just before it landed and his laughter immediately died. For a second she thought he might be mad when she realized he had a different look of intensity in his eyes.

As if on cue, her body tingled in response. "Don't look at me like that. I was serious."

"Look at you like what?" he asked as he approached her.

She took a few steps back. "Like you want to—uhh—"

"I do," he said, the hunger in his voice now as intense as the look in his eyes.

"But what about—"

"Babe. You aren't going to get fleas." He pressed his body against hers, walking them both backwards until the backs of her knees hit the bed and he pushed her down and followed right after. "Unless you spend all your time in wolf form and stop bathing, you have nothing to worry about."

"That's even if I turn. There's still a chance I won't, right?"

He licked across the bite marks on her neck, his new favorite spot, and then looked up at her. "You are definitely going to turn. Soon."

"How can you be so sure?" she asked breathlessly.

He used his legs to push hers open and pressed his cock against her opening. Before she had a chance to gather her wits, he pushed inside her, causing her to gasp. He hadn't lied when he said it would fit, but it was so much. It nearly robbed her of breath.

"Babe, I am one hundred percent sure because your eyes are glowing."

"What?" she cried out, clawing at the bedsheets. "Let me—" Her request to see them died as he began to move. Lightning struck and whatever else she wanted to know would have to wait.

"Dante," she whispered on the little breath still left in her body.

"I know, babe. Me too." No more words were spoken as they rode out the pleasure together for what seemed like hours. Her body would be sore, but she didn't care. Her body pulsed with more than just a release. The emotion he unleashed in her flooded out and by the time they were finished neither one of them could move.

"I love you, Rebel," he whispered in her ear as he rolled them to their sides with him still locked inside her.

"I love you, too."

EPILOGUE

D*iego*

Faith, Damien, Rebel and Dante were all gathered around the table in his dining room when Diego walked through the door. The table was covered with every kind of breakfast food known to man and his stomach growled at the sight.

He eyed the piles of meat and contemplated where he would start.

"I hope you plan to save some for me," he said. He hopped into one of the empty chairs and grabbed a plate.

After picking out about ten slices of bacon, he dug into the pile of eggs and glanced up to find them all staring at him.

"What?" he asked, shoveling more food in his mouth.

"Oh I don't know," Damien started. "Last time we saw you, you were walking away with our captured hunter and no one has seen you for over twenty-four hours. Where is she?"

"In the basement. Where do you think? I've been interrogating her." He stuffed two pieces of sausage in his mouth and reached for the pancakes.

They all eyed him suspiciously, which he chose to ignore. As much as they wanted to talk about her, he did not. The situation was going to be a lot more complicated than any of them suspected.

In the hopes of distracting them, he changed the subject. What they didn't know wouldn't hurt them.

"So you two finally did it, huh?" he said, looking over at Dante and Rebel. Not that it wasn't obvious. The bonding pheromones cloaking them were still fresh and fucking with his brain. "Guess you were wrong about the true mate thing, too."

"What?" Rebel nearly choked on her food.

"The bond. I can sense it. Can't you?"

Rebel turned to Dante and he simply grinned, shaking his head. Apparently he had not gotten around to telling her yet.

Somewhat amused by his brother, but still on edge from his own encounter, he took a deep breath and focused on the food in front of him. He'd been too busy to eat and he had some catching up to do.

"That's it? You're not going to tell us what happened with her?" Faith asked.

He shrugged. So much for distraction. "Sure, I guess. Her name is Allison Fox and she's from Seattle. Her brother Brody was supposedly attacked and bitten by a wolf either here on the island or nearby. Now he's missing and she is hunting him and prepared to take out any shifter who gets in her way. So... Needless to say, I've got her locked up until we can find her brother who is probably our rogue wolf."

Dante's disbelieving eyebrow popped up. "It took you twenty-four hours to get that little?"

"More or less." What was he supposed to say? He wasn't about to tell them the truth. At least not all of it. They only had one more night of mating season to go and then he could wipe this mess clean.

No one needed to know he was already addicted to a woman trying to kill him.

⟨∘◦◉◦∘⟩

Thank you so much for reading!

READY TO CONTINUE with more Devils Point Wolves? Mating Season isn't quite done and Allison and Diego are about to get their worlds turned upside down. Check out **WANTED, available now.**

Join Eliza's VIP newsletter at elizagayle.com/newsletter and be the first to be notified of new releases, sales and contests.

If you enjoyed this story please take a moment to help other readers discover it by leaving a review on your favorite retailer.

Just a few words and some stars really does help!

If you're on Facebook or Twitter, come by and say hello! I'd love to hear from you.

Continue reading for a bonus chapter from WANTED, the next book in the Devils Point Wolves series (now available) and the full booklist from Eliza Gayle.

SNEAK PEEK FROM WANTED

By

Eliza Gayle

Copyright 2015

All Rights Reserved

Book Description:

This mating season has one last trick to play...

Allison Fox is on the hunt again. Except this time the werewolf she's been assigned to track is her brother. The search has led to the island of Devils Point and it doesn't take her long to figure out she's hit the mother lode—of werewolves. But when she meets Diego, her world turns upside down.

As mating season comes to a close, Diego is thrown into chaos when he's given the task of interrogating the female hunter who would like nothing more than to kill him. His track record with women sucks and this one is no better. Especially when his wolf stands up and claims her as his mate.

BONUS CHAPTER - WANTED

COMPLETE 1ST CHAPTER - WANTED

Allison Fox twisted in the sand, putting the handcuffs holding her wrists underneath her and came face to face with a devil. A dark eyed, dark haired gorgeous devil at that whose every tall, muscled inch towered over here. Despite the scowl and the danger emanating from him, the man underneath intrigued her.

She recognized her captor as Diego, one of the brothers who owned Club Diablo. A strip club that sat at the entrance to Devils Point, the island these men called home.

Except these were no ordinary men. They were dangerous werewolves who threatened humanity with their very existence. Although they were nothing like the wolves she'd encountered in the past. These were clean, well dressed and rather articulate. It hadn't been easy identifying them as shifters at first.

Except this was their mating season, the one time a year they lost control when it came to their need to mate. And with such single-minded focus distracting them, they tended to let their guards down.

"You got her, Diego? Or do you need our help getting her home?"

She turned to the voice to see Dante and Damien also staring down at her. Although they were shifting around as if antsy to get the hell out of there.

"Not much to it. Look at her. She's like a scrawny rat. I can handle her alone."

Scrawny rat. She took offense at his assessment of her but kept her mouth firmly shut. The less she engaged the better. Besides, her energy was better used to figure out her escape. She still had a mission to accomplish before she could go home.

"Good, we're headed back home to check on the others. But Chess and Branch will be around if you need some help."

Diego leaned down and grabbed her around the shoulder and hauled her to her feet. Effortlessly she noted. No small feat for her one hundred and seventy pounds. He might have compared her to a scrawny rat, but she was far from it. Thanks to her family genes she was stocky at best and overweight at worst. And no diet in the world seemed to change that.

"Let me go," she demanded, wrenching her arm free from his hold.

"No," Diego said.

"Have fun little brother. Don't forget to call if you need some help handling her." Both men disappeared into the woods amidst guffaws and snickers. Whatever was so funny she didn't understand.

"You can't hold me like this. I have rights."

He glared at her, the intensity in his eyes allowing some of her fear to get the better of her.

"You gave up your rights when you tried to shoot my brother." Diego wrapped his hand around her arm just above the elbow and steered her in the direction his brothers had gone.

Handcuffed and having been divested of all of her primary weapons, even the small hunting knife she kept in her boot, she had no choice but to go with him and hope as time went on she'd discover a way to break free and then make these wolves pay.

"Why did you try to shoot him?"

"He's a werewolf. Why wouldn't I?"

"That's a shitty answer."

Allison shrugged. "It's the truth."

He stopped and hauled her close. So close there was barely a breath between them and she immediately felt his body heat. And his scent. It didn't take supernatural anything to identify the woodsy outdoors mixed with the spice of his soap. It was a heady mix.

More than that. He was somehow screwing with her brain. She couldn't exactly focus on anything but him and how good he felt this close to her.

She planted her hands on this chest and tried to push away. "Whatever you're doing to me stop it. I don't do wolves and getting inside my head won't change that."

"You don't do wolves." He repeated her statement very slowly and with a low growl behind it. "And how exactly am I getting in your head? I haven't even begun to interrogate you."

"I don't know," she said, shaking her head. "I just know something's not right and you must be the cause of it."

He rolled his eyes and continued his trek, pulling her along with him. "You're nuts and I don't mean that in some cute way like you humans think. I was at a party, minding my own business. I sure as hell didn't need this shit tonight. I mean look at that moon. Do you even know what that means?"

"Your mating season is coming to an end?" She glanced up at the near full moon shining unbelievably bright in the sky and took a scientific guess based on what she'd been taught.

"How do you know that?" he demanded.

"Just lucky I guess."

He shook his head and she heard that low growl again. "This is not how you want to play it with me tonight. I'm already on edge. Having to deal with you isn't helping."

"This isn't exactly a party for me either. These handcuffs are digging into my wrists and I'm being dragged deep into the woods by a beast. Last time I checked that doesn't bode well for me."

"This isn't a horror movie. I have no cabin in these woods where I take nosy, dangerous humans like you and slaughter them."

She stumbled before righting herself. "But you do have a home out here?" she asked.

"Yeah, the one you shot up earlier. I live there with my brother."

Interesting. "Sounds like you and your brother are close."

"We are. Which is why I'm a little put out that you tried to kill him tonight."

"If I had tried to kill him he would be dead. I haven't missed a shot like that since I was twelve and learning to shoot."

Diego whipped around and she crashed into him face first considering the top of her head barely came to his shoulders. This was no ordinary crash though. Never in her life had she landed on such a finely sculpted wall of muscle. The few guys she'd let get this close were not built like this. Athletic yes, extraordinary specimens, no.

"Would you please stop doing that?"

His chest rumbled under her cheek. "What's wrong, little girl, are you afraid of the big bad wolf?"

"Hardly. I just have no need for you in my personal space."

He shifted closer and she could have sworn for a fleeting second he was hard. And this time she wasn't referring to his chest or abs. Allison sucked in a breath.

For a few long seconds neither of them spoke and all she heard was the roaring of her pulse in her ears. Or maybe it was the erratic and wild tempo of her heartbeat. No, she wasn't exactly afraid of the wolf, but this wasn't like her previous encounters and she couldn't explain why being so close to this one made her heart beat double time or her body ache.

"Get in," he ordered.

She blinked and looked up at him, not entirely sure she heard him correctly.

"What do you—" He nodded his head to the right and she turned to see he was directing her toward a dark, open topped jeep with big tires on it that were great for mudding.

"Uhm, no thanks," she said. "I don't take rides from strangers."

He sighed and wrapped his hands around her waist and lifted her where he wanted her. A pulsing shock of electricity coursed through her at his touch. For a second all she could focus on was that tiny contact and by the time enough of her wits returned to focus, he was already walking around the vehicle and getting in.

"I demand you let me go." She was beginning to panic. Between the weird unexplained reactions to his touch and the fear of being held captive in some wolf lair, she had to exert some control into the situation.

"I wanted a carefree party and maybe a dick sucking tonight. I guess neither of us is going to get what we want."

Her brain tripped and melted. His vulgar reference to oral sex should have pissed her off or at the very least grossed her out at the image that painted in her head.

So why had the ache in her chest suddenly traveled south. Not once had anyone in her family mentioned that wolves had special pheromones that could ensnare her. But why else was she having such a visceral reaction to a man like him? He was supposed to be disgusting and bloodthirsty and a danger to human society.

She wasn't supposed to want to screw his brains out within five minutes of meeting him.

Obviously unaffected or unaware of what was going on with her, he started the engine and took off.

Read more WANTED now

ALSO BY ELIZA GAYLE

The Dragon Lore Trilogy:

THE CURSE OF THE DRAGON

THE SOUL OF THE DRAGON

THE FIRE OF THE DRAGON

Southern Shifters Series:

SHIFTER MARKED

MATE NIGHT

ALPHA KNOWS BEST

BAD KITTY

BE WERE

SHIFTIN' DIRTY

BEAR NAKED TRUTH

ALPHA BEAST

ONE CRAZY WOLF

Enigma Shifters Fated Mates:

DRAGON MATED

WOLF BAITED

BEARLY DATED

WOLF TEMPTED

Devils Point Wolves:

WILD

WICKED

WANTED

FERAL

FIERCE

FURY

Single titles:

VAMPIRE AWAKENING

WITCH AND WERE

WRITING AS E.M. GAYLE
CONTEMPORARY ROMANCE

Mafia Mayhem Duet Series:

MERCILESS SINNER

SINNER TAKES ALL

WICKED BEAST

WILLING BEAUTY

BROKEN SAINT

FALLEN ANGEL

Outlaw Justice Series:

SAVAGE PROTECTOR

RECKLESS PAWN

RUTHLESS REDEMPTION

Outlaw Justice: Sins of Wrath MC:

CRUEL SAVIOR

SCORCHED KING

VICIOUS DEFENDER

Purgatory Masters Series:

TUCKER'S FALL

LEVI'S ULTIMATUM

MASON'S RULE

GABE'S OBSESSION

GABE'S RECKONING

Purgatory Club:

ROPED

WATCH ME

TEASED

BURN

BOTTOMS UP

HOLD ME CLOSE

Pleasure Playground Series:

PLAY WITH ME

POWER PLAY

Single Title:

TAMING BEAUTY

WICKED CHRISTMAS EVE

Gypsy Ink Books
www.gypsyinkbooks.wordpress.com